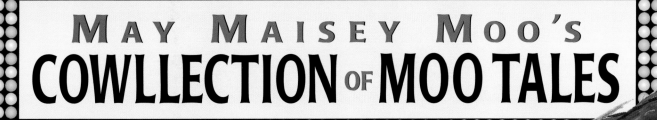

MAY MAISEY MOO'S
COWLLECTION OF MOO TALES

VOLUME I
THE COWVENTION

Created and Written by

VIN ESOLDI

Illustrations by

ROBERT BOURDEAUX

Produced and Designed by
Trez Cattie Pomilo

Original Characters by
Robert Leighton and Vin Esoldi

Paula Press Publishers
Clinton, NJ

In Loving Memory...

This book is dedicated to Fran Schwartz, Anne Mitchell,

Margaret Wittman, Bill Masi, Bruce Bordelon and my Mother Moo,

Mary A. Esoldi, who are all in the company of my

favorite holy cows, Helen and Scarlet, enjoying that

hayvenly pastureland above.

A cowlossal "thank you" to my cheerleading team here

on terra firma...Bob Bourdeaux, Trez and Jim Pomilo, Robert Leighton,

Lou Dorff, Lyn Mackie, Sue Proctor, Michael Dorff, Joyce and Art

Ostrin, Ray Toscano, Judy Sabo Podinker, Diane Laurent, Joanie and

Pete Backes, Bill Cressler, Nancy Goldberg, Kathy West, Karen B.

Katzel, Ilona Smithkin, Steve Jenkins, Maureen Broglia, Jack Mullen,

Peter O'Donnell, Aunt Frances and Uncle Al Pepe and all my family

and friends who were there for me when "the skies got gray

and the herd was a-runnin' every which-a-way."

Mooo.... *Vin Esoldi*

PAULA PRESS PUBLISHERS
PO Box 5057
Clinton, New Jersey 08809-0057
877-870-COWS (2697)

First Edition 1999
10 9 8 7 6 5 4 3 2 1

Library of Congress Card Catalog Number:

99-96031

ISBN: 1-929745-00-1

Manufactured in the United States

"What a moovelous day for our Cowvention," thought May Maisey. "I can't wait to see everyone!"

Ms. May Maisey Moo, the famous Broadway star heifer and cow-about-town, was serving as the hostess with the moostest at this International Gathering of Celebrated Cows.

May Maisey was particularly excited that she would once again see some of her close friends who would be traveling here from far and near. There would be Madame Foo Moo from China, CowMoo Mooranda from South America, Mama Mooa from Italy, Moozambica from Africa, Mooaghondi from India, The Queen Mother Moo from England, and Moo's dear, dear friend, Mademooselle Moo Moo Moonel, the famous hat designer from Paris, France.

Aside from hostessing the Cowvention, May Maisey was also serving as a delegate from the eastern part of the United States. She hadn't met the other three U.S. delegates — Mooria Moo from the Midwest and Southwest, Magnolia Moo from the South, and Malibua Moo representing the West. Of course there would be many other cows representing many other countries as well.

"Oh dear," thought May Maisey. "How will I ever remember who's who? I have such a terrible moomory for names. Well, no time to worry about that now. My friends will be here soon."

Anticipating an udderly hectic schedule once the Cowvention started, May Maisey arranged for her friends and other U.S. delegates to arrive early and meet in a separate room not far from the main hall where all the delegates would later assemble.

The first to arrive was Mooaghondi from India.

"Mooaghondi, it is so famoobulous to see you," said May Maisey. "How was your trip?"

"Oh, May Maisey, the flight from India was lovely indeed, but trying to get here from the airport was quite another matter. I informed the taxicab driver that I wished to be driven to the Cowvention Hall and instead he drove me to the Cow Palace...dear me, I thought I would be so late, but I see that I am the first to arrive."

"Ola, Ola, Ola May Maisey, Ola Ola Ola Mooaghondi. It is I, CowMoo, CowMoo Mooranda. Mirame! Miramoo! Hugs and smooches! Hugs and smooches!"

With that dramatic greeting, a vision of ruffles and feathers, sequins and spangles, fruit and froufrou was seen gliding across the lobby floor.

"What a joy it is to see you, and what a deliciously moolicious outfit," said May Maisey as she hugged CowMoo.

"You like? I designed it myself," said CowMoo.

The next to arrive was Mama Mooa, who brought gifts with her of homemade pasta and jars of tomato sauce. "Mama always travels with food," she proclaimed.

She was followed by Moozambica and Madame Foo Moo. Since they were staying at the same Red Barn Mootel, they shared the same taxicab.

"What a contrasting picture they make," thought May Maisey. Foo Moo was short and petite and dressed in an outfit of delicate, soft, embroidered silk and pearls. Moozambica was tall and very stately in her brightly hand-dyed garments and her big bold jewelry of amber and ebony.

Everyone politely bowed when the Queen Mother Moo arrived, but she very quickly waved everyone to return to their normal standing position.

"Oh, me, Oh moo, I get so embarrassed with all this bowing, especially when my friends do it," said the Queen.

"Moo Cherie, Moo Cherie — it is sooo divinely bovine to see all of you here. I have designed you special hats for this lovely occasion."

"My dear Moo Moo, thank you so much, what an absolutely hayvenly thing to do!" said May Maisey as she warmly greeted her close friend, Mademooselle Moo Moo Moonel, from Paris, France.

The cows spent the next hour chewing the cud and mooing about this and that. Mooaghondi spoke about her latest visit to the wondrous Taj Moohal in her native India.

The Queen Mother Moo had likewise just completed a tour of the many cowlossal castles in her Moorrie Olde England.

With all this talk of moonuments, Mademooselle Moo Moo Moonel decided it would be moonificent to have a replica of the Eiffel Tower on her next hat creation.

CowMoo Mooranda demonstrated a few dance steps she would do in her next show, the Cow-a-Bongo Moosical Revue. Moozambica inquired if there would be any entertainment after the Cowvention was over. She was assured by May Maisey that the wonderful Mooettes, featuring Dolly, Holly and Polly McMoo, would moo a moodley of their best-loved songs.

While Mama Mooa and Madame Foo Moo were explaining to all some of their great recipes, such as Moozarella Clover and Moo Moo Gai Pan Hay, the group was joined by the other U.S. delegates-- Malibua Moo, Magnolia Moo and Mooria Moo.

May Maisey introduced them to everyone present and inquired about their trips to the Cowvention.

Malibua had traveled east with her husband, Muscle Moo Bulky Bull, and their flight was as smooth as milk.

Magnolia Moo had stopped at Moobile to visit her dear Aunt Moozella before coming to this great gathering. "What a lovely trip this has been," she mooed to one and all.

M ooria Moo had traveled by car with her husband, the extremely famous wrestler, Bull "Mountain Moo" Doorham, and said it was great fun seeing many of America's cow fields that they had never seen before.

While all the cows were chatting away, there was a sudden, frantic knock at the door. May Maisey hardly had the door open when in rushed Moovana, the Chaircow of the Cowvention.

"Mooo, May Maisey! Mooo, May Maisey! Whatever are we to dooo, May Maisey?" Moovana cried out. Everyone was startled and instantly silenced by poor Moovana's anxious plea for help.

"Dear girl, please calm down!" exclaimed May Maisey. "Whatever it is, we'll all try to help, but you'll have to calm down so you can tell us precisely what has happened."

"Oh me, oh moo, what a disaster, what a disaster!" the poor heifer hollered. "What are we to do, what are we to do?"

May Maisey put her arm around Moovana, trying to calm her down. "Moovana dear, we can't help you unless you tell us what disastrous event has occurred!"

"Well," Moovana began, "I just returned from a meeting with Mr. Grizzle Grrrunt, the new owner of the Cowvention Center. He said that the moola we paid to Mr. Gladhand Goodlyoink, the previous owner, for our three-day Cowvention was not enough, and that if we don't come up with more moola by tomorrow morning, he would kick us out! Whatever are we to do?" Moovana wailed.

"How much more moola does he seek?" queried Mooaghondi.

"Two hundred thirty-four thousand, five hundred sixty-seven dollars and eighty-nine cents!" Moovana emphatically proclaimed, as if the amount was etched in her hide.

"Why, that greedy little pig!" retorted Mooria Moo.

"Well, cornstarch my cud! If it's that porker I saw earlier today," exclaimed Magnolia Moo, "there's nothing little about that over-stuffed sausage!"

Calling him names will get us nowhere, thought May Maisey.

"What about the contract you signed with that dear Mr. Goodlyoink?" May Maisey asked of Moovana.

"Mr. Grrrunt is not going to honor it," wept Moovana, "and now there's not even enough time to hire a lawyer and go to court."

"Maybe we can make an emergency cash cowllection among the delegates?" suggested Madame Foo Moo. "Then we can go to court later on and teach that greedy hog a lesson or two."

"That's a barnbastic idea," said May Maisey. "Let's start the cowllection right here in this room"

Every cow there dug deep into purses and pockets, looking for any pennies, pences, or pesos they might have to contribute.

When all the cold cash was carefully calculated, the moola added up to only one hundred and two dollars and thirty-four cents!!

"We are twelve cows," mulled May Maisey, "and that is all we could cowllect...how can that be?"

"Moo cherie, who carries cash anymore?" sighed Mademooselle Moo Moo Moonel. "Except for the moolala we use for taxis and tips, everything else can be purchased with credit cards; alas, we are no longer--how do you say?--cash cows!!"

"How about wiring for more moola from our home pasturelands?" queried Moozambica.

"It's too late," answered Moovana. "The banks are closed. It's the weekend. The Cowvention is doomed, doomed!" she cried.

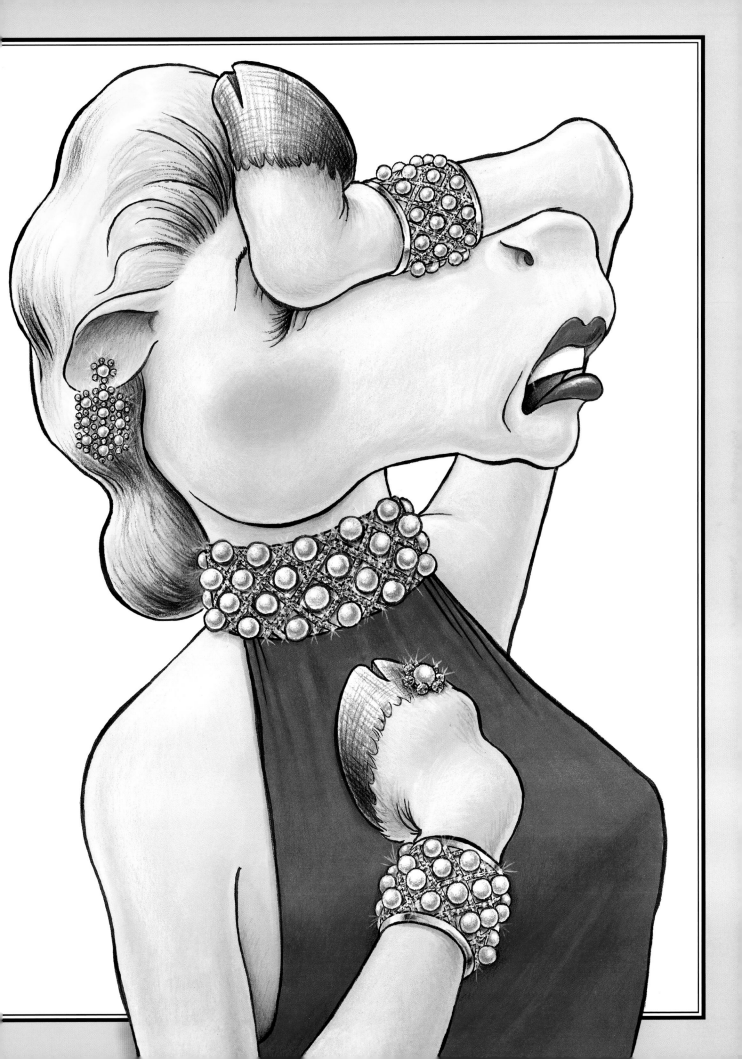

"Now, now, brown cow," said the Queen Mother Moo. "We may all come from different parts of the world, look different, dress differently, and have different interests and occupations, but that is no reason why we can't put our horns together and come up with a solution to the dilemma. I know we can do it!"

"Lalalala laada!
Lalalala laada!"

Åfter such a stirring speech, silence once again fell upon the cows. Everyone was deep in thought trying to find a solution.

After a few minutes, the silence was broken by CowMoo Mooranda, who, while trying a second time to count the moola cowllected, inadvertently started humming one of the tunes from her new moosical revue... *"Lalalala laada! Lalalala laada!"*

Then Mama Mooa, ever so deep in thought, started beating her bread-sticks on the table as if she were beating a drum. *"Boomboomboom boom boombang! Boomboomboomboomboombang!"*

Clickclick
ickclick
lack!"

That was followed by Madame Foo Moo sliding her jade rings up and down her long pearl necklace. *"Clickclickclickclick click-clack!"*

It wasn't long before Moozambica was banging together her ebony bracelets and May Maisey was tapping her hoofs, as if she was ready to do one of her stage numbers of long ago.

One by one, the cows realized what was beginning to happen. With all of the humming and drumming, clicking and clacking, slapping and tapping, a moosical symphony of sounds issued forth — a beat that stirred the heifers from horn to hoof.

While everyone was having such an udderly moovelous time singing and dancing and carrying on with glee, it dawned on May Maisey what could be done to raise the additional moola that Mr. Grrrunt demanded.

They could have a moosical concert — right here — in the Cowvention Center —that night!! Sell tickets — cash only!! After all, they did have the stage, the chairs, the lights, the mikes and the moopower.

There already were some performers present for the Cowvention and, with all the show-business cownnections these mooers and shakers had, they could easily get more performers to appear if their schedules allowed.

"We can do it!" shouted May Maisey. "We can get a concert together by tonight!" She was frantically running around trying to stop the Cowga line, the singing, the dancing, the mooing and the merriment. "We can raise the cash, pay the piggish Mr. Grrrunt and have a moovelous time doing it as well!" she shouted. "All we need is teamwork...so let's get started. We haven't much time!"

Soon after May Maisey's plan was discussed, all the cows divided themselves into cowmittees. One herd called top-name performers they knew to see who was available to perform; another called the police department to get the permits they would need and also to arrange for herd control; yet another would deal with the radio and television news announcements for their benefit concert.

Even Mama Mooa pitched in by setting up all the food and catering needs to feed the anxious performers and busy backstage crew.

In record time, through the herdwork of all the cows involved in this team effort, announcements were being made, tickets were being sold, and the cash was coming in to ensure that the Cowvention would continue all weekend.

Now it was time for this lovely cowl-lection of moo tails to leave the private room that May Maisey had set aside for them and join the other guests.

They joined the thousands of other cows who had traveled there from all over the world and who were now assembled in the Cowlossal Cowvention Center.

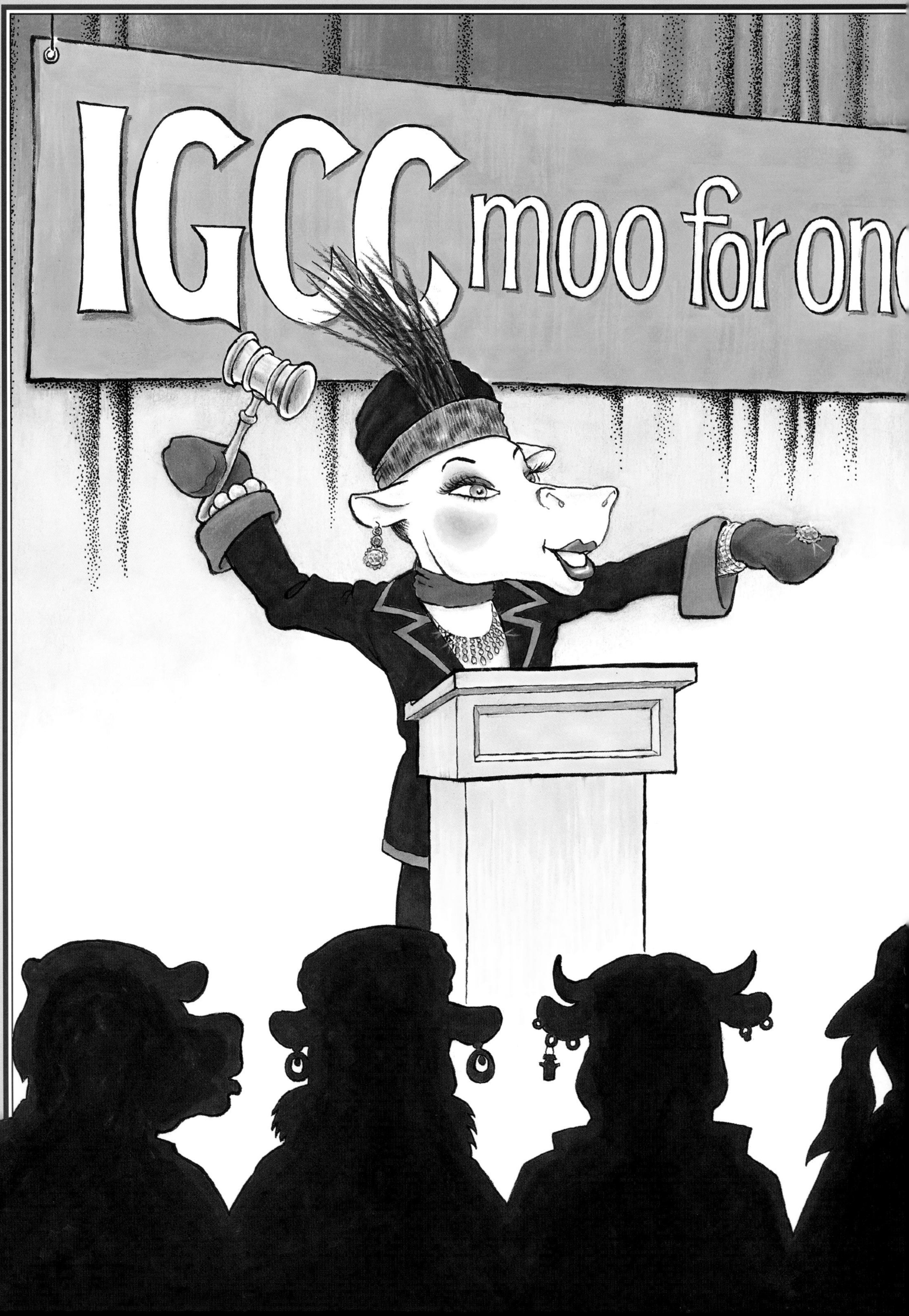
IGCC moo for on

moo for all

Since the anticipation for that night's concert was running high, the first day's session of the Cowvention seemed to fly by very quickly.

With the last bang of the gavel officially closing the session, May Maisey and her friends made a stampede to the backstage area so that they would be there in time to greet the arriving performers.

Surprisingly, the first performer to arrive was Moomoona. Her usually late arrivals were legendary in the world of entertainment. Already in costume, and with her hidedresser busily tweaking her golden locks, Moomoona was quickly ushered down the hall to her dressing room.

"May Maisey, doll!" Moomoona mooed halfway down the hall. "You look fabu, simply fabu! Smooches, smooches!!"

"Thank you, dear...and thank you for helping out," May Maisey mooed back. "We'll chew the cud later and have a fabmoobulous chat."

"What an...exotic outfit she had on," commented the Queen Mother Moo.

"Oui, oui, yes, yes," Mademooselle Moo Moo agreed. "I think her designer is from my beloved Paree."

☙

Cow Belle Clowie and Billy Bud Bull, the famous country crooning couple, were the next to arrive. They were greeted by their close friends, Mooria Moo and her husband Bull "Mountain Moo" Doorham.

"Like, thanks for doing this," gushed Mooria. "I can't believe you were both available...and on such short notice!"

"Anything for good friends," said Billy Bud. "And for a good cause!" added Cow Belle. "It must have been fate that we were available to perform tonight," she continued, "because our only other plan for the evening was to stay home and watch a rerun of 'Moo Over Miami'."

By now, some of the press was allowed backstage for pictures and short interviews. No sooner had they arrived when a huge entourage accompanying the gorgeous Hayleeta appeared at the stage door.

Suddenly, flashbulbs were going off everywhere and questions were being shouted out like crazy. "Who was...?" "When was...?" "Could you...?" "Would you...?" "Did you...?" etc., etc., etc.

❧

Finally, May Maisey decided it was time to rescue Hayleeta from the media moohem. She darted over to Hayleeta and whisked her away to her dressing stall.

Once inside, May Maisey was finally able to give her a proper greeting.

"My dear, dear Hayleeta. You look absolutely moognificent. Motherhood must agree with you. How is your precious little Bovinia?" asked May Maisey.

"She's just the cutest calf in all of Clover County," glowed Hayleeta. Just then, there was a knock on the door.

"May Maisey, Miss Moot's here," a voice hollered out on the other side of the door. "Miss Moot Moovis is here."

"Thank you, I'll be right there," May Maisey assured them.

"Oh me, oh moo, is that crazy cow also performing here tonight?" joked Hayleeta. "Well, you give that girl a big hug and smooch from me." And with that said, Hayleeta batted her big beautiful bovine eyes as May Maisey blew her a smooch goodbye and told her she'd see her later, after the concert.

Once outside Hayleeta's dressing stall, May Maisey could see that Moot Moovis had not only arrived...but was indeed holding court with the reporters and cameramen.

May Maisey thought to herself, Only Miss Moot, oh excuse me, The Bovine Miss Moovis, could wrap that group of press people around her little hoof!

"Oh, Maisey, there ya are, girl! What keptcha? I've been entertaining the troops here--right, boys?" and with those words Miss Moot went into one of her famous vampish poses and the flashbulbs popped like crazy.

"Easy boys, easy," joked Moot, "I want to be able to see tonight."

May Maisey shook her head and gave Moot a big hug. "I was just in with Hayleeta," said May Maisey, "and she sends her love."

"Well, mymymymymymymy moo, how is that cowlossally rich chanteuse doing? And now she's a mother to boot. Holy Cow, what a gal she is, what a pal...I can't wait to see her later for a few udderly chewy chew chuckles," Moot responded.

"Let me show you to your dressing stall," suggested May Maisey, "so you can start getting ready."

"Ready? Ready? Girl, I'm always ready! Isn't that right, boys?" joked Moot. "Well, actually I could use a little time to...powder my snoot. Ta, ta. Now, boys, get ready for one last picture pose!"

And with that, Moot just kept waving and waving goodbye, throwing smooches to one and all.

With the flashbulbs still popping, she and May Maisey walked down the hall to her dressing stall.

As Moot entered her stall, Moovana, the Chaircow of the Cowvention, came rushing toward May Maisey.

"Oh, May Maisey, good news...we did it, we did it, we've sold out the concert!" proclaimed Moovana.

Before Moovana could even finish her next sentence, May Maisey immediately started doing one of her old "soft-hoof" dance routines.

As all of her friends gathered around to applaud the good news, Moovana started waving her arms and mooing, "Wait, please, wait, there's more to tell. There's bad news as well!

"We sold out the concert, but we're still short on the moola that Mr. Grrrunt is demanding."

"How short?" all the anxious cows queried in unison.

"Seven thousand, six hundred fifty-four dollars and thirty-two cents," responded Moovana. And with that said, she started boo-mooing again.

"Now, now, Moovana, we've come this far...have faith! With a little Bovine intervention, I'm certain that all the moola we need to raise will somehow, by some cow, be raised!!" said May Maisey.

"Five minutes, five minutes 'til show time," hollered the Stage Manager. As the excitement mounted, Moovana and the rest of the cows took their assigned seats.

At first May Maisey felt that she should stay backstage and try to come up with a solution to the shortage of funds. But she soon realized that there was no sense in worrying herself sick, as she would probably wind up with a stomach ache...and for cows, who all have four stomachs, that's not a very wise thing to do!

So May Maisey decided to join the others in the audience and enjoy the concert like everyone else. And enjoy the concert she did!!

When it was over, all the cows suddenly jumped to their hooves. A thunderous applause was given by this very pleased herd of heifers.

Moovana, May Maisey, and all their friends rushed backstage to congratulate and thank all the performers, moosicians and volunteers who helped make the concert a huge success.

On the way to the backstage area, they all decided not to mention to anyone that they were still short of funds. After all, this was such a wonderful mooment, and everyone had worked so hard to make it a success. It would be a shame to burst everyone's bubble of enthusiasm.

As May Maisey and her friends greeted everyone, a herd of officials and policemen, led by Mr. Goodlyoink, headed their way.

"Oh, Moovana, oh, friends," huffed and puffed Mr. Goodlyoink, "what an evening, what a turn of events, what a story for the press! When the police got your frantic calls for the concert-permit requests and were told the reason for this last-minute fundraising," he continued, "they started getting suspicious about Mr. Grrrunt and his peculiar demands. After investigating him, they soon found out that there was more to that pig than meets the sty. He's a fraud and a cheat, and was going to leave the country with the cash he demanded from you and your Cowvention.

"Now I'd like you all to meet the Honorable Judge Hoot Owland. He's declared the sale of the Cowvention Center null and void, and so, for the time being, I'm still considered the owner," said Mr. Goodlyoink. "I'm so sorry for all the stress you've gone through today, so I want you all to know that not only will you be able to keep the proceeds from this evening's event, but I will also be donating the use of the Cowvention Center for the entire weekend and will be sending back your rental fees paid so far."

There was a dead silence as all the Moo Cows' jaws dropped in udder shock.

However, it wasn't too long, before everyone started to cheer and shout, holler and whoop, sing and dance.

Once again, a Cowga dance line was formed, only this time it was made up of all those backstage...May Maisey and her friends, the performers, Mr. Goodlyoink, Judge Owland and the policemen, with even the moosicians and stagehands joining in. Someone raised the curtain and the Cowga line spilled onto the stage.

The Cowvention continued for the next two days--and although many, many important issues were raised and many important problems solved, for May Maisey and her friends, the time moost fondly remembered would be the successful concert and then all the partying that went on...

...'TIL THE COWS WENT HOME!!!

GLOSSARY OF MOO-WORDS

Barnbastic	fantastic
Boo-Mooing	crying; "boo-hooing"
Bovine	pertaining to cows
Chaircow	chairperson, or, more accurately, chairwoman
Chanteuse	a female singer or a singer in nightclubs or cabarets
Cowga Line	similar to a line dance like the "Conga Line"
Cowllection (cowllect)	collection, collect
Cowlossal	colossal, grand; on a large scale
Cowmittees	committees
Cow Palace	a famous entertainment arena
Cowvention	convention
Fabmoobulous	fabulous
Fabu	abbreviation for fabmoobulous, like "fab" for fabulous
Froufrou	excessive ornamentation or trimming
Hayvenly	heavenly
Herd Control	crowd control
Hidedresser	hairdresser
Mademooselle	Mademoiselle: French for "Miss"
"Mirame, Miramoo"	Spanish for "Look at me"
Moobile	Mobile, a city in Alabama
Moo Cherie	bovine for the French "ma cherie" or "my dear," a greeting
Moodley	medley
Moohem	mayhem; confusion; turmoil
Moola	money
Moolala	bovine for oo-lala or "how wonderful"
Moomory	memory
Moo Moo Gai Pan Hay	a bovine version of the Chinese meal Moo Goo Gai Pan
Moonificent	magnificent
Moonuments	monuments
Moo Over Miami	a reference to the song "Moon Over Miami"
Moorrie	merrie: old-fashion spelling of "merry," as in "Merrie Olde England"
Moosical	musical
Moosicians	musicians
Moost	most
Moostest	bovine slang for the "mostess," as in "the hostess with the mostest"
Mootel	motel
Moovelous	marvelous
Mooers and Shakers	movers and shakers; those who make it happen
Moozarella	Mozzarella: a cheese
"Ola"	Spanish for "hello"
Paree	Paris, the capital city of France
Pasturelands	homelands
Soft-Hoof Dance	soft-shoe dance
Smooch	kiss
Taj Moohal	Taj Mahal, a palace built for royalty in Agra, India
Udderly	utterly; completely, totally or absolutely
"What keptcha?"	What kept you? (What delayed you?)